A story about God's power. . .
and about trust.

It Happened at Mackey's Point

by Jane Belk Moncure
illustrated by
Lydia Halverson

Published by The Dandelion House
A Division of The Child's World

for distribution by **VICTOR** ─────────

BOOKS a division of SP Publications, Inc.

WHEATON. ILLINOIS 60187

Offices also in
Whitby, Ontario, Canada
Amersham-on-the-Hill, Bucks, England

Published by The Dandelion House, A Division of The Child's World, Inc.
© 1984 SP Publications, Inc. All rights reserved. Printed in U.S.A.

A Book for Competent Readers.

Library of Congress Cataloging in Publication Data

Moncure, Jane Belk.
  It happened at Mackey's Point.

  Summary: A family's sugar beet business is wiped
out by a cyclone, but they continue to trust in God's
wisdom and, in time, something good comes out of the
devastation.
  [1. Christian life—Fiction] I. Halverson,
Lydia, ill. II. Title.
PZ7.M739It 1984   [E]   84-7039
ISBN 0-89693-220-6

1 2 3 4 5 6 7 8 9 10 11 12 R 90 89 88 87 86 85 84

It Happened at Mackey's Point

Mackey's Point was a long, narrow piece of land, pointing like a giant finger into a great lake. One side sloped gently to the water's edge. The other side was washed by a river as it flowed into the lake.

The farmhouse stood on a hill overlooking the lake. It was here Josh lived with his mom and dad and Grandpa Mackey. The Mackeys raised cattle on the high pasture. They grew sugar beets on the lowlands between the lake and the river.

By the time Josh was seven, Grandpa said he could do a man-sized job. There were plenty of man-sized jobs to do like fixing fences, feeding cattle, and stacking firewood for winter. But there was also time for fishing.

Josh had his own boat. He knew every cove along the lake shore for miles around. Grandpa knew even more. He knew where the big fish hid.

"Throw your line near that old log," he would say. "There's a hungry fish looking for his dinner. Let's catch him for *our* dinner."

Most of the time they did. But once in a while, a really big fish got away.

Josh thought Mackey's Point was the most won-
derful place in the world. His favorite spot was a
waterfall about a mile up the river. Sometimes, on
hot summer days, Josh and Grandpa Mackey would
hike there. They would sit on a rock below the falls
where they could feel the misty spray as the water
tumbled by.

"It's so powerful," said Josh one day.

"God's great power is all around us, Josh. If we
look for it, we can see it in all His creation."

Josh had another favorite place. It was his tree house by the lake. Sometimes on quiet, summer evenings, Josh and Grandpa would climb into the tree house after sunset. They'd watch the sky fill up with stars.

"Did God make every star?" Josh asked one night.

"God—in His mighty power—made the whole universe," whispered Grandpa. "He made everything in it—the stars, the waterfalls, the lakes. . . ."

"Even the fireflies?" asked Josh.

"Even the fireflies."

As Josh stood close to his grandpa, he wished that everything would always stay the same at Mackey's Point.

One summer, however, everything changed. The usual rains did not come. There were days and weeks of hot weather.

"It's the worst dry spell I can remember," said Josh's mom.

"It's a good thing we live between the lake and the river," said his dad. "We can pump water to our sugar beet fields and save our crops." And they did. Week after week they pumped water onto the beet fields.

Then, in early September, the air became sticky and hot. One evening when the sunset was a strange dull color, Grandpa said, "There's a storm

on the way. I can feel it." By evening the news
came over the radio:

"Storm warnings for all points along the lake."

"It may be a dangerous storm," said Dad.

"Could be very dangerous," said Grandpa. "Years ago a big storm blew through here and flooded the farm. Lake waves rolled in as high as ocean waves."

"Let's get the cattle into the barn. Hurry," called Dad.

"Tie up the boats!" shouted Grandpa.

"Help me get the porch furniture inside," called Mom.

Finally everything was secured. The last stray cow was safely in the barn. The family bolted the door and waited for the storm.

But they didn't wait for long. Suddenly the wind
and rain came with great force. Trees bent so low
their branches swept the ground like giant brooms.
Wind swirled and knocked down fences and tel-
ephone wires. The electricity went out. Everything
was dark.

Josh was frightened. Grandpa put his arm around
Josh. "I know how you feel," said Grandpa. "Sometimes I'm afraid too. But you know, God is always
with us—even in the middle of a storm. Josh, the
storm is another proof of God's power."

Then Grandpa started singing a hymn Josh liked:
"God Will Take Care of You." Mom lit a candle.
Then they all sang together. After awhile, Josh fell
asleep in Grandpa's arms.

For hours that night the lake waves rolled over
the meadow, across the beet fields, and into the
river on the other side of Mackey's Point. Finally
the lake and the river became one big lake.

By morning, the terrible storm had passed. The monstrous wind had become a playful breeze. But Mackey's Point had changed forever. It was under a foot of water.

"Everything's ruined! My tree house is gone," sobbed Josh. "And my boat! My boat is gone too."

Grandpa stood beside him. "It's a pitiful sight and I'm sure sorry. Lots of things are ruined and gone. But, Josh, not everything. Surely not everything. Look. We are safe. We should thank God. We can fix things. . .but people. . .we can't fix people."

"But why did God let this happen?" asked Josh.

"God's mighty power is shown in ways we don't always understand. But one thing I'm sure of—God will give us the strength we need if only we ask Him and trust Him. Now we'd better get going. Your dad needs us down at the barn. We've man-sized jobs to do today."

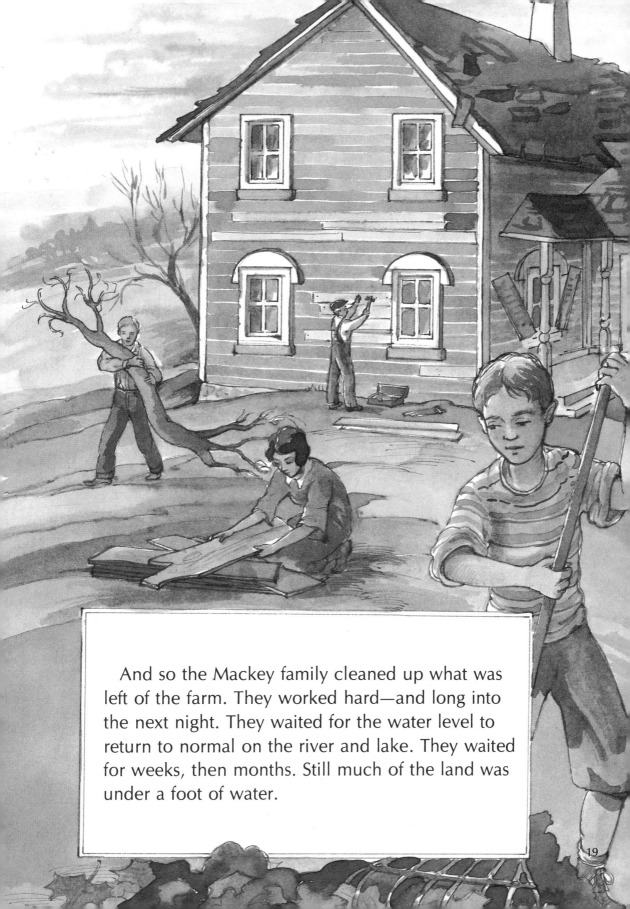

And so the Mackey family cleaned up what was left of the farm. They worked hard—and long into the next night. They waited for the water level to return to normal on the river and lake. They waited for weeks, then months. Still much of the land was under a foot of water.

19

"I'm afraid the lowland has become one big useless marsh," said Dad one November afternoon.

"More like a giant mud puddle," said Josh. "Good for nothing."

"I wouldn't be too sure," said Grandpa. "That marsh may be good for something. God works in mysterious ways. He has the power to take things that seem bad and turn them into something good."

"I know something *you* can be good for, Josh," called Mom. "How about bringing in some logs for the fire?"

All that first winter after the storm, the family struggled to make a living. With the beet crop gone, they began selling lumber. It was hard work, cutting down trees and sawing boards.

When Josh looked at the marsh, he wanted to cry. Everything looked stiff and dead. Even the few cattails that had sprung up now stood frozen in the ice.

There wasn't much money for Christmas that
year. But Grandpa surprised Josh with a new tree
house behind the barn.

And the family enjoyed Christmas day together.

"We have each other. And a Christmas dinner," said Mom.

"And plenty of firewood," said Dad.

"And come spring, we can plant a new beet field," said Grandpa. "I think this family might sing praises to God for seeing us through this very tough time."

Grandpa started singing, "Praise God from Whom All Blessings Flow."

Josh didn't sing at first. He wondered to himself, "Does God really care? Can He help us through this terrible time? Grandpa has faith. He even thanks God for biscuits and milk gravy."

And by the end of the song, Josh was singing too.
Still it was a very hard winter.

By April the farm was alive with the beauty of God's creation. The plants and flowers told of His glory. Even the marsh was blooming with cattails, marsh grass and pond weeds. A neighbor loaned Josh a rowboat. The first warm Saturday Josh paddled the boat across the marsh.

Suddenly he noticed two little reddish-brown animals swimming among the cattails. They looked like small beavers but their tails were different. Josh called them marshlings.

Josh didn't think much about the marshlings until later in the summer. That was when he discovered some little dome-shaped mounds of pond weeds near the edge of a bank. He counted several mounds here and there among the cattails.

Early in the fall, Josh and Grandpa saw Canadian geese flying into the marsh by the hundreds. They came to feed on the marsh grass and pond weeds.

"How did the geese know about our marsh?" asked Josh.

"Instinct," said Grandpa. "God made animals and birds so they have special ways of knowing many things. Besides, plants are growing in the marsh now—good food for geese." And he winked as he continued, "God is changing that marsh into something good. What did I tell you?"

And on Thanksgiving Day when Mom baked a goose for dinner, Grandpa said a special thank you to God for the geese and the marsh.

Yet as winter settled in, the marsh looked lifeless again. Even the little mounds of mud and cattails all around the banks looked cold and barren.

But no one knew what was happening inside those mounds. And in the springtime, even Grandpa was surprised to see the marsh nearly full of splashing marshlings. The little creatures dived here and there among the cattails.

"I'm going to get Bruce Bradley down here to have a look at our marshlings," said Grandpa. "Bradley is the best trapper in these parts. He will know what our marsh visitors are."

Bruce Bradley knew right away.

"Why, you've got yourself a muskrat farm. Yep, a ready made muskrat fur farm. The water is just the right level. And cattails are a feast for muskrats. Man, you're in business, the fur business. How about a job?"

"We thought our land was ruined," said Dad.

"Good for nothing but cattails," said Mom.

"I told you that God in His great power can take something we think is bad and turn it into good,"

said Grandpa Mackey, chuckling. "I've been around for 78 years. That's long enough to know that God works in ways we don't always understand. But if we have faith, God is powerful enough to give us strength to carry on—and work things out for the better somehow. That's His *mighty power!*"

This story is true. And for years the Mackey family has raised muskrats. Their beautiful fur goes by many names like "water mink," "river fur," and "lake sable." It is made into warm coats and jackets for people all around the country.

If you drive by Mackey's Point today, you will see a sign above the marsh.

Josh is now grown up and has a grandson named Josh. If you stop for a visit, maybe Josh III will take you for a ride around the marsh in his new rowboat.